SUPER DC HEROES

BATMAN

THE REVENGE OF CLAYFACE

WRITTEN BY
ERIC STEVENS

ILLUSTRATED BY
GREGG SCHIGIEL AND
LEE LOUGHRIDGE

BATMAN CREATED BY
BOB KANE

Raintree

(R) www.rai ...
Visit our w ...
more info
Raintree b ...   b.co.uk
c ...

"Raintree" is a registered trademark of Pearson Education Limited, under licence to Capstone
Global Library Limited

First published by Stone Arch Books in 2009
First published in hardback in the United Kingdom in 2010
Paperback edition first published in the United Kingdom in 2010
The moral rights of the proprietor have been asserted.

Art Director: Bob Lentz
Designer: Brann Garvey
UK Editor: Vaarunika Dharmapala
Originated by Capstone Global Library Ltd
Printed and bound in China by Leo Paper Products Ltd

ISBN 978 1 406215 45 8 (hardback)
14 13 12 11 10
10 9 8 7 6 5 4 3 2 1

ISBN 978 1 406215 59 5 (paperback)
14 13 12 11 10
10 9 8 7 6 5 4 3 2 1

British Library Cataloguing in Publication Data
A full catalogue record for this book is available from the British Library.

CONTENTS

CHAPTER 1

PARABOMB X

Billionaire Bruce Wayne rushed through the lobby of his office building Wayne Tower. He pushed the button for the lift and looked down at his watch. "Late again," Bruce mumbled to himself.

The billionaire was used to being late. His secret identity as Batman, Gotham City's greatest crime fighter, often kept him from his business duties as the head of Wayne Enterprises. Today was different, though. He had an important meeting with a group of high-ranking military officials.

The officials were going to demonstrate the prototype of a secret, high-tech weapon. Bruce didn't want to keep them waiting.

The lift doors finally opened. Inside stood a large security guard, wearing a bullet-proof vest and carrying an automatic rifle. "Good morning, Mr Wayne," said the guard, recognizing his employer.

"Morning, Jenson," Bruce replied and stepped inside the lift. "Have all my guests arrived for the meeting?"

"All except one, sir," said the guard. He scanned a list of names on a clipboard. "General James Werther."

At Bruce's request, the security guard pressed an unmarked button on the lift's control panel. The doors slowly began to close.

Then suddenly, a hand reached in and stopped them. The guard readied his rifle as the doors opened up again. A man in a military uniform stood on the other side.

"It's okay, Jenson," Bruce said. He shook the man's hand. "Thank you for coming, General Werther. I'm Bruce Wayne."

The general stepped inside, and the guard again pressed the unmarked button. This time the doors closed. The lift sped towards the top floor of the skyscraper.

"Glad I'm not the only one that's late," said Bruce. He jabbed the general with his elbow and gave him a joking wink.

The general's face reddened as he looked up at Bruce. A bead of sweat rolled down his balding scalp and onto his nose. "I, um, was held up," said the general, nervously.

"Don't worry," Bruce said with a smile. "I'm sure they didn't start without us."

Just then, the lift stopped, and the doors slid open. The guard led the men into a large meeting room. Inside, the top officials from each branch of the Armed Forces sat at a long table. At the end of the table stood the Secretary of Defence, gazing out of a row of large, glass windows.

"We've been waiting, Mr Wayne," said the Secretary without facing the billionaire.

"I'm sorry, Mr Secretary," Bruce apologized. "We can start right away."

"Good," snapped the Secretary. He motioned for the guard to join him at the front of the table. Bruce sat at the other end, awaiting the demonstration. General Werther joined the other officials.

As the men waited, the security guard swung his automatic rifle over his back. He bent down near the Secretary, picked up a metal case on the floor, and placed it on the table.

The guard and Secretary both removed large keys from around their necks. Each placed their key into a slot on the side of the case, and then gave them a turn. **CLICK! CLICK!** The lid of the case slowly opened.

The Secretary reached inside and pulled out a gleaming, silver ball. A single green button on top of the sphere pulsed like a beating heart.

"Gentlemen," the Secretary began. He held the sphere out towards Bruce Wayne and the wide-eyed officials. "I present to you . . . the ParaBomb X."

CHAPTER 2

CLAYFACE

"Very impressive, Mr Secretary," said Bruce. "But I've never been in the business of funding weapons."

"I assure you, Mr Wayne," the Secretary replied, "this weapon is unlike any other. It is extremely powerful but not deadly."

The Secretary told the guard to dim the lights. Then, he pressed the glowing green button on the sphere. Suddenly, it split in half, hinging open like a metal jaw. A bright green light flared out from inside the sphere, colouring everything in the room.

"I have the ParaBomb in safe mode, so this light cannot harm us," the Secretary continued. "In combat, however, it could paralyze every enemy on the battlefield."

"And what about your own troops?" Bruce interrupted.

"Safety glasses," said the Secretary, tossing Bruce a pair of high-tech sunglasses. The guard handed out pairs to the military officials as well. "These are specially made to resist the ParaBomb's effects."

"And can the paralyzing effects be reversed?" asked Bruce.

"Yes," the Secretary replied. "We've developed a highly effective antidote. Of course, the formula is top secret."

"Any other questions?" the Secretary said, looking around the room.

For a moment, the room was quiet. Then something in the room started to grumble like a loud, hungry stomach.

Bruce looked over at General Werther, who had been late to the meeting. The general was sweating again, and his face was as red as blood.

"I have a question, Mr Secretary," he growled. "Have you ever seen a general fly?" General Werther stood and jumped onto the boardroom table.

"Werther!" yelled the Secretary. "What do you think you're doing?"

The general reached down and picked up a pair of the special safety goggles. Then he ran down the length of the table, grabbed the sphere from the Secretary's hands, and leaped towards the windows.

Glass shattered, and the general plummeted toward the ground below.

"He'll die!" one of the officials cried.

Bruce shook his head. "I don't think so," he whispered to himself.

As General Werther slammed on to the street, his body suddenly changed. He was not a general anymore. Instead, he was a big lump of soft, muddy clay.

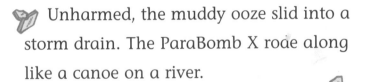 Unharmed, the muddy ooze slid into a storm drain. The ParaBomb X rode along like a canoe on a river.

"How did he do that?!" yelled the Secretary of Defence. "Guards, call an all-points bulletin on General Werther!"

"Good idea," Bruce said. He stealthily picked up a pair of the special sunglasses and headed for the lift.

"Where are you going, Mr Wayne?" asked the Secretary. "The General just stole the world's most powerful weapon!"

"Exactly," Bruce replied. He stepped into the lift and pressed the button for the lobby. "I have to secure my building." The lift's doors closed. *And I must stop Clayface,* Bruce thought.

After a moment, the lift reached the lobby. As Bruce rushed towards the building's front doors, he pulled out his mobile phone. "Call home," he said into the high-tech device.

Seconds later, his trusted butler, Alfred, answered. "Yes, Master Bruce," he said.

"Alfred, we've got trouble," said Bruce. He walked through the revolving doors of Wayne Tower on to the street.

Bruce pushed through a crowd of onlookers that had gathered outside. He stared into the empty storm drain. "Clayface has stolen a new weapon, right from under my nose," Bruce told Alfred.

"That doesn't sound like his typical crime, sir," Alfred replied. "He's not a thief."

"Exactly," Bruce said, puzzled. "So what's he up to?"

"Perhaps this might help, sir," Alfred said. "A source has just informed me of a very unusual meeting tonight."

"A meeting?" Bruce asked.

"Yes, sir," Alfred continued. "A number of crime bosses are gathering tonight at the abandoned warehouse on Bay Boulevard."

"The old sporting goods shop?" Bruce asked.

"The very same," Alfred replied. "Perhaps Clayface will be attending."

Bruce nodded. "Of course," he said. "He'll offer the weapon to the highest bidder. Still, this isn't normal for Clayface."

"Even criminals out for revenge need money, I suppose," Alfred suggested. "He has to eat while he hunts for Daggett."

"True," Bruce replied.

He thought about the man named Matt Hagen who had become Clayface. Hagen was once a famous, handsome movie star before a crash left him horribly disfigured. Hagen learned about a dangerous chemical invented by a man named Roland Daggett. Daggett promised that the chemical would make Hagen handsome again, and it did.

But soon, the two men fought.
Then Hagen consumed too much of the
chemical, and his entire body began to
change. He was no longer human. He
was transformed into the hulking menace
known as Clayface. And Daggett became
the target of the mudman's twisted hatred.

"Thanks, Alfred," Bruce added. "And I
might be a little late tonight. I have a party
to crash."

"Of course, sir," the butler replied. "I'll
put your dinner in the fridge."

Bruce switched off his mobile phone.
He ran back into Wayne Tower to change
into the Batsuit. "I'm getting a little tired of
reheated meals," he mumbled.

CHAPTER 3

TRICKED!

A few hours later, Batman crouched on a rafter in the abandoned sporting goods warehouse. He waited in the shadows for the criminals to arrive. As the minutes passed, Batman started to think Alfred had received some false information.

Then suddenly, the big double doors of the warehouse swung open. Several men walked in, laughing and joking. "What's this meeting all about?" said one of the men. "My boys and I have a bank robbery planned for tonight."

"If this guy doesn't show quick," another said. "I'm going to start some trouble."

"Nice group," Batman whispered from his perch above.

After a moment, one more man walked into the warehouse. In his hand was a large, black briefcase. He was wearing a pair of sunglasses, which were much too small for his huge, muddy face.

"Clayface," Batman said to himself. "Now, it's a party."

"Finally," snapped one of the crime bosses. "What's in the case?"

"Yeah, Clayface," another man said. "And what's with those ugly sunglasses?"

"This?" Clayface said, holding up the briefcase. "This is a dream come true – at least for one of you."

Clayface placed the case on a small table in the centre of the room. The bosses gathered around their hulking host.

"What is it?" one criminal asked, leaning in for a closer look. "Are you trying to sell it?"

"That's right," Clayface replied. He lifted out the ParaBomb X. Its green, pulsing light glowed brightly throughout the room. "And it goes to the highest bidder."

Batman shifted a little on his perch. "Something's not right," he said to himself. "Why is Clayface wearing the safety glasses if he's trying to sell the weapon?"

Clayface placed the metal sphere on the table. "Let's start the bidding," he said. "What will you give me for this unstoppable weapon?"

"Weapon?" said one of the crooks. "We don't even know what it does!"'

Clayface threw his giant hands up. "Of course!" he said. "How about a demonstration?" His deep voice sounded like a muddy gargle.

High above, Batman pulled the extra pair of sunglasses out of his Utility Belt and slipped them on. "Good thing I grabbed these," he said to himself.

The bosses all gathered around the sphere. "That's right! Everyone move in close," Clayface said.

The mudman smiled and pressed the glowing green button. "Here goes," he said.

The sphere hummed loudly and clicked open. A bright light shone out from inside, covering the entire warehouse.

"Hey, what is this?!" one of the bosses started to say. The next second, he and the others fell to the floor, paralyzed.

For a moment, Clayface stared at the crime bosses, lying helplessly on the cement floor. He reached down and closed the sphere. Clayface stood in the darkened warehouse, amazed by the weapon's awesome power.

THE CLOWN PRINCE OF CRIME

Batman took off his special sunglasses and got ready to pounce on the mud-faced criminal. At the same time, Clayface pulled off his sunglasses as well. Then he turned towards a side door of the warehouse.

"All clear!" yelled Clayface.

Batman froze. He watched the doors of the warehouse open again. The shadow of a man appeared.

"Well done, my pottery pal," a familiar voice said from the doorway.

The man stepped out of the shadows. His white face glowed brightly in the dim light of the warehouse. He smiled crazily from ear to ear. "Joker," Batman growled.

"Are they really paralyzed?" asked the Joker. He walked towards a crumpled crime boss and gave him a swift kick. The crime boss didn't even flinch.

"They're all out cold, Joker," Clayface said. "Trust me."

"Trust?" Joker replied. "It's so important, isn't it? When I asked you to steal the ParaBomb X, you trusted me, didn't you?"

"That's right," Clayface said. "Because you promised me Daggett. Where is he?"

"Ah, yes," the Joker replied. "Roland Daggett, your nemesis. Remind me, why exactly did you want him?"

Clayface approached the Joker. "You know why!" he shouted. He towered above the Joker, spitting mud into his face. "He's the man who turned me into a freak!"

"Don't you trust me, Clayface?" Joker said. He leaned over the weapon. He ran his hands over the shiny surface of the sphere. "How long will these mugs be out cold?"

"Until they're given the antidote," Clayface growled. Batman could hear the anger in the mudman's voice. "Now where's Daggett?"

"So impatient," Joker said. He closed the case and picked it up.

"Hey, what is this?" Clayface said. "You're not taking the weapon until I have Daggett." He lunged at the Joker.

"Time to move," Batman said.

Batman leaped down from the rafters and kicked Clayface in the chest. Surprised, the hulking mass of mud fell back against the wall. His special, high-tech safety glasses fell to the floor.

"Drop the weapon, Joker," Batman ordered, spinning towards the crazy crook.

The Joker laughed. "Not this time, Batman," said the Clown Prince of Crime. "Clayface, if you want Daggett, you'd better get this winged freak away from me!"

Clayface quickly rose from the floor. His white eyes glowed red with anger. Suddenly, his arms started to grow and stretch. His hands formed into giant hammers. He swung them through the air at Batman in a violent flurry of mud.

"Good job," Joker said, as Batman jumped to avoid the attack. "Now, I'm afraid you'll have to excuse me." The Joker picked up the sunglasses from the floor. He ran through the door and hopped into his waiting Jokermobile.

"You won't get away with this, Joker!" Clayface shouted.

He turned towards Batman. "This is your fault! I nearly had my revenge, and now the Joker is gone!" cried the madman. He rushed after Batman again, swinging his giant hammer arms.

Batman dodged quickly to the right. *SMASH!* One of Clayface's giant hammer arms crashed to the ground. Batman dodged to the left. *SMASH!* The other hammer thundered to the floor, crashing through the solid cement.

Batman knew he couldn't avoid the heavy blows much longer. He waited for just the right moment. Then he dashed between the mudman's hulking legs.

For a moment, Clayface's giant arms kept thrashing. Their incredible weight was nearly impossible for the mudman to stop.

Meanwhile, Batman ran through the warehouse doors. The Caped Crusader dived into his Batmobile and flicked on the afterburners. With a sudden jolt, the car quickly reached maximum speed.

Clayface watched as the Batmobile took off after the Jokermobile. "Come back here!" he shouted in anger.

Then suddenly, the hulking mud-covered criminal transformed his shape again. This time he became a clay tank. He raced down the city streets after the other two cars.

Meanwhile, Batman zoomed after the Jokermobile. "Alfred," he said. The Batmobile's wireless transmitter opened communication with his butler at the Batcave. "I'm in pursuit of the Joker."

"The Joker, sir?" Alfred asked. "I thought you were after Clayface."

"The Joker was behind the whole thing," Batman said. "He's got the ParaBomb X, and his strongest criminal competition are out cold on the warehouse floor."

"I'll notify the police, sir," Alfred said.

"Good, they can clean up the mess at the warehouse," Batman replied. "And I'll take out the trash."

CHAPTER 5

THE RIVER OF DEATH

Batman sped through the streets of Gotham City. Soon, he was right on the tail of the Jokermobile. The Joker took a sharp left turn, careening over a pavement and plowing through a newspaper stand. Fortunately, it was empty.

"Maniac," Batman muttered. He picked up speed and followed closely behind. He swerved to avoid other cars and frightened pedestrians.

Then suddenly, Batman heard a loud smash, and the Batmobile began to shake. He gripped the steering wheel tight to avoid losing control. *WHAM!* The car shook again. "What's going on!" Batman yelled.

"Give up now, Batman!" a gravelly voice called out from behind. "You won't get away from me!"

Batman glanced in his rearview mirror. It was Clayface. He was right behind the Batmobile, swinging huge hammers from the top of his tank-like body.

The Caped Crusader turned the Batmobile sharply down an alley. Clayface tried to follow, but the alley was too narrow for the giant tank. Batman's move gave him a few extra seconds to speed after the Jokermobile.

Soon the Jokermobile had reached the entrance to the Trigate Bridge. "He's heading out of Gotham City," Batman muttered.

Batman hit a switch on the dashboard. Rockets flared, and the Batmobile suddenly shot forward. He sped past the Joker on to the bridge. Then, Batman cranked the steering wheel. The car spun around, stopping sideways and blocking both lanes.

Quickly, Batman jumped out of the Batmobile. He pulled out his grappling hook from his Utility Belt, and he fired it at the Jokermobile's tyre.

The sharp, metal point of the hook pierced the rubber tyre. The Jokermobile squealed and spun, then hit the kerb and rolled over.

SMASH! The car slammed into the steel railing on the side of the bridge. It crashed through the beam and came to a sudden stop. The Jokermobile teetered on the edge of the bridge, a hundred feet above the dark river.

"Help!" the Joker cried through the open window. "Help me!"

Batman strode towards the Joker's car. "Hello, Joker," he said calmly. "You look a little on edge."

"Get me out of here!" the Joker snapped.

"I don't know," Batman said. "If I open this door, you'll slide out, right into the river."

"Then do it carefully," the Joker replied angrily, "and catch me before I fall!"

Batman swung open the door and grabbed the villain by the foot. At the same time, the ParaBomb X fell off the car's seat, bounced onto the street, and rolled over the edge of the bridge.

"My new toy!" the Joker cried. He reached for it, but it was too late. The ParaBomb X splashed into the river, sinking quickly in the murky water.

Batman pulled the Joker to safety. "That could have been you," he said. "Besides, it's better off at the bottom of the river."

Batman dropped the Joker into the Batmobile's passenger seat. Then he activated the prisoner constraints. Heavy straps and buckles kept the Joker from escaping. "That should hold you until I can get you back to Arkham Asylum," Batman said.

Suddenly, the bridge began to shake. Batman braced himself against the railing. A rumbling started, getting louder by the second. Moments later, Clayface appeared, thundering toward the Batmobile. His giant clay feet shattered the ground with each angry step.

"Hand over the Joker," he said. "He still owes me Daggett!"

Batman crouched as Clayface got closer. "You won't get your revenge today, Clayface," he said. "I doubt the Joker ever had Daggett at all!"

Clayface roared and charged ahead. Batman stayed crouched, ready to fight or leap. Just as Clayface was nearly on top of him, Batman dived to one side. He flipped once and landed out of Clayface's way.

Clayface tumbled over and over, rolling toward the bridge's railing. He couldn't stop in time, and the railing was no match for the mudman's huge bulk. He crashed through the steel beam and fell helplessly into the river.

Batman ran to the edge of the bridge. He watched as Clayface hit the water and instantly began to dissolve.

• • •

Back at Wayne Manor that night, Bruce Wayne sat down to his reheated supper. Alfred ladled some soup into a bowl and placed it in front of Bruce.

"Thank you, Alfred," Bruce Wayne said. "This looks great."

"So, is that the end of the ParaBomb X, sir?" Alfred asked, serving the soup.

Bruce took a sip from his soup. He wiped his mouth and placed the napkin beside him on the table.

"For now," he said. "I'll retrieve the sphere from the river tomorrow and hide it in the Batcave. I also told the Secretary of Defence that I'm pulling out of the project. It's too easy for the orb to fall into the wrong hands."

"Wise choice, sir," Alfred said. He poured some water and handed it to Bruce. "Although the bomb did you a favour by knocking out a warehouse full of criminals. What happened to the Joker, sir?"

"He's back in Arkham," Bruce replied, taking a long drink. "I don't know how long it will hold him this time."

"And Clayface, sir?" asked Alfred.

Bruce set the glass of water down and stared at it. "Clayface fell into the Gotham River. I watched him dissolve," he said.

Water seemed so harmless, but it was the one thing that Clayface could never withstand. Bruce folded his hands in front of him and gritted his teeth.

"It sounds terrible," said Alfred. "Let's hope that will be the end of Clayface."

Bruce pushed back his chair and stood up. He walked to the dining room window and gazed at Gotham City's midnight skyline. A dark, dirty rain had started to fall. "I can't help thinking that we haven't seen the last of Mr Hagen," Bruce said quietly.

"Why's that, sir?" asked Alfred, clearing away the dishes.

"Clayface is out for revenge," said Bruce.

As he said that, Bruce thought about his own parents and how they had died at the hands of a criminal. He thought about how their deaths had eventually led him to become Batman. "Revenge," he added, "is hard to kill."

Clayface

REAL NAME: Matt Hagen

OCCUPATION: Professional criminal

BASE: Gotham City

HEIGHT:
Varies

WEIGHT:
Varies

EYES:
Varies

HAIR:
Varies

Formerly a big name in the film industry, actor Matt Hagen had his face, and career, ruined in a tragic car crash. Hoping to regain his good looks, Hagen accepted the help of ruthless businessman Roland Daggett, who gave him a special cream that allowed Hagen to shape his face like clay. Hopelessly addicted, Hagen was caught stealing more cream, and Daggett forced him to consume an entire barrel as punishment. However, instead of killing Hagen, the large dose turned him into a monster with only one thing on his muddy mind: revenge.

- As Clayface, Matt Hagen is no longer human. His entire body is made of muddy clay, which grants him shapeshifting abilities as well as super-strength.

- Clayface's power is limited only by his imagination. He can turn his limbs into lethal weapons by willing his muddy body into whatever shape he desires.

- Everything Clayface does revolves around his relentless pursuit of Roland Daggett, the man who made him into a freak. Clayface will do whatever it takes to get Daggett within his muddy grasp, regardless of who is hurt or killed in the process.

- Drawing upon his shapeshifting abilities and his experience as an actor, Clayface assumes the shapes and voices of others. These abilities make him a very difficult foe to detect.

CONFIDENTIAL

BIOGRAPHIES

Eric Stevens is studying to become an English teacher. Some of his favourite things include pizza, playing video games, watching cooking shows on TV, riding his bike, and trying new restaurants. Some of his least favourite things include olives and shovelling snow.

Gregg Schigiel has wanted to be a cartoonist since he was 11 years old. Schigiel has worked on projects featuring Batman, Spider-Man, SpongeBob SquarePants, and just about everything in between.

Lee Loughridge has been working in comics for more than 14 years. He currently lives in a tent on the beach.

GLOSSARY

afterburners devices that increase the speed of something

antidote something that stops a poison from working

careening swerving or lurching while in motion

formula recipe for creating something

nemesis opponent or enemy of a person

paralyze make someone lose the power to move

prototype first version of an invention that tests an idea to see if it will work

shattered broken into tiny pieces

stealthily secretly or quietly

transformed made a great change in something, or turned into something else

Utility Belt Batman's belt, which holds all of his weaponry and gadgets

DISCUSSION QUESTIONS

1. Clayface is angry because Roland Daggett made him into a monster. Does this excuse his evil behaviour? Explain your answer.

2. The Joker is one of Batman's most dangerous enemies. Why do you think the Dark Knight saves him from falling into the river? Would you have done the same? Explain.

3. At the end of the story, Clayface dissolves in the river. Do you think he will ever return? Why or why not?

WRITING PROMPTS

1. Batman and the Joker both have high-tech vehicles. Describe your own dream vehicle. What colour would it be? How fast would it go?

2. Write your own story about Batman and Clayface. Who will Clayface transform into next time? How will Batman capture him again? You decide.

3. Many books are written and illustrated by two different people. Write a story, and then give it to a friend to illustrate the pictures.